WITHDRAWN

Oliver

TO ALL THOSE WHO HAVE EVER FELT A BIT DIFFERENT

WITH ENDLESS THANKS
TO MY FAMILY

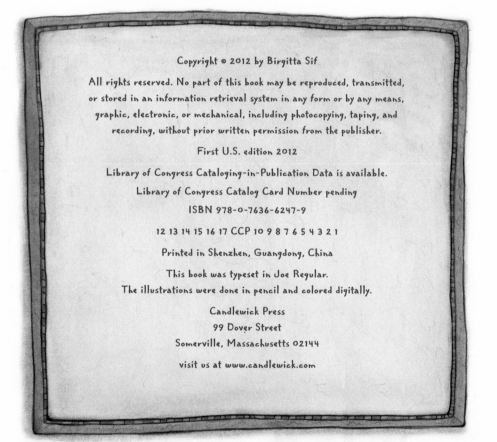

First U.S. edition 2012

Library of Congress Cataloging-in-Publication Data is available.

Library of Congress Catalog Card Number pending

ISBN 978-0-7636-6247-9

12 13 14 15 16 17 CCP 10 9 8 7 6 5 4 3 2 1

Printed in Shenzhen, Guangdong, China

This book was typeset in Joe Regular.
The illustrations were done in pencil and colored digitally.

Candlewick Press
99 Dover Street
Somerville, Massachusetts 02144

visit us at www.candlewick.com

CANDLEWICK PRESS

Oliver

BiRGiTTA SiF

Oliver felt a bit different.

But it didn't matter.
He lived in his own world,
happily, with his friends.

They had lots of adventures together.

They searched for treasure and rode camels through the desert.

They crossed narrow bridges and bravely fought sharks.

They jumped over oceans and slid down waterfalls.

They even visited the other side of the world.

But sometimes there were
things Oliver had to do
on his own.

And sometimes, wherever he was,
he wanted to fly away.

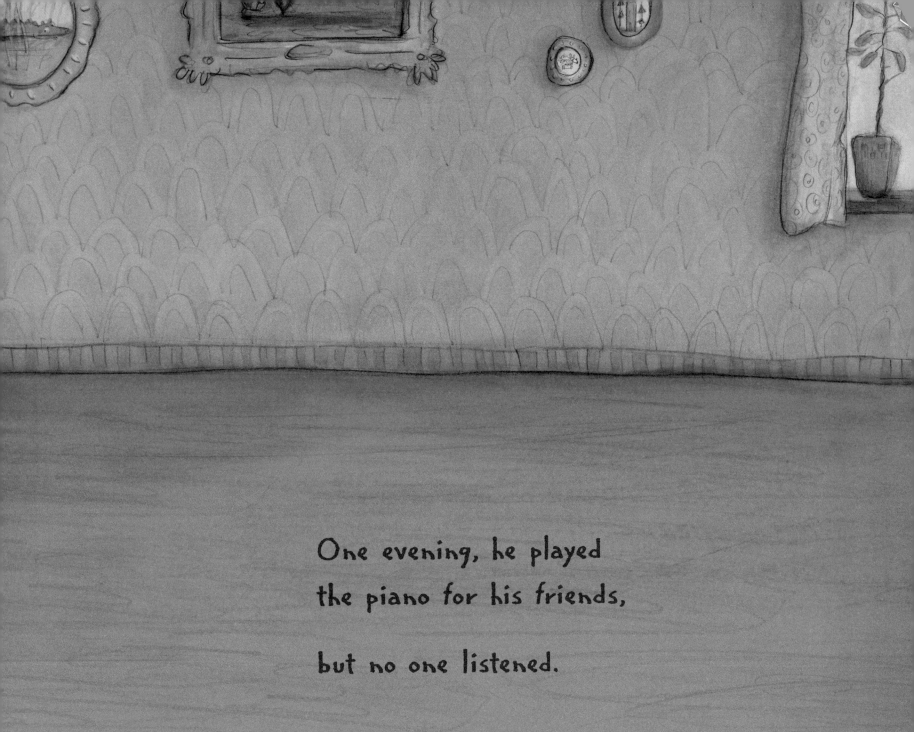

One evening, he played
the piano for his friends,

but no one listened.

Oliver felt a bit different.

The next day, as he was
playing tennis on his own . . .

the ball flew over his head...

and bounced . . . and bounced . . . and rolled . . . and rolled away.

So Oliver set off on
another adventure,

through the wild jungle,
over the river,

up and up
the mountain,

until he found a narrow gate
to somewhere new.

It was the beginning of the
best adventure he'd ever had.

Oliver was a bit different.

But it didn't matter.

Olivia was
a bit different too.